THE
GREENS
FIND THEIR
SPACE

PAGE PUBLISHING, INC.
New York, NY

First originally published by Page Publishing, Inc. 2017

ISBN 978-1-68348-819-4 (Paperback)
ISBN 978-1-64082-884-1 (Hardcover)
ISBN 978-1-68348-820-0 (Digital)

Printed in the United States of America

THE GREENS
FIND THEIR SPACE

Jymi Bond

Ken and Kelly worked as vegetable farmers.

They grew corn, potatoes, and carrots.

Their farm was huge, and they wanted
to plant a new vegetable.

"Greens," Kelly said. "We'll start with collards and go to kale. What we don't eat, we can sell."

The plan went well. The weather was no fail,
and the bugs didn't eat the crops away.

Then came the day the
greens made their way above ground.

Corn from the beginning,
was curious about the new neighbor.

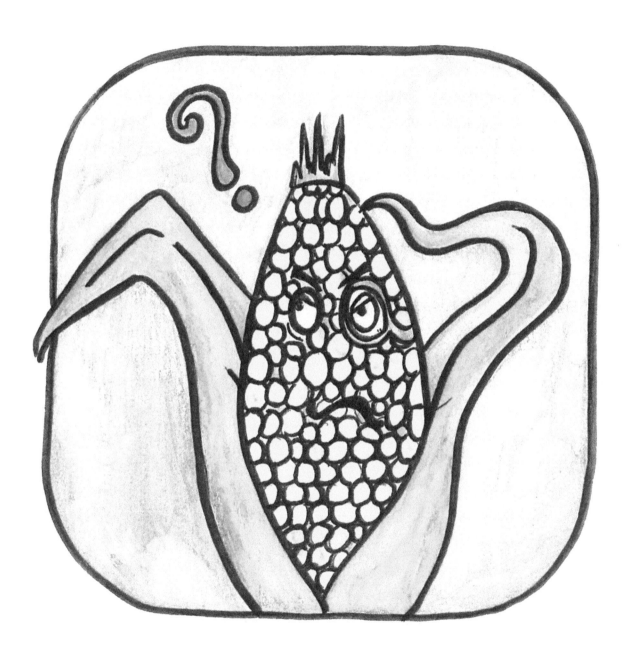

"What are you, and what do you do?"
Corn snarled and went on to say…

"I am Corn, made from the sun, and I have many uses—too many to name—but food is my claim to fame, and I am taking other offers. Again, I say, please forgive my rude way, what do you do?"

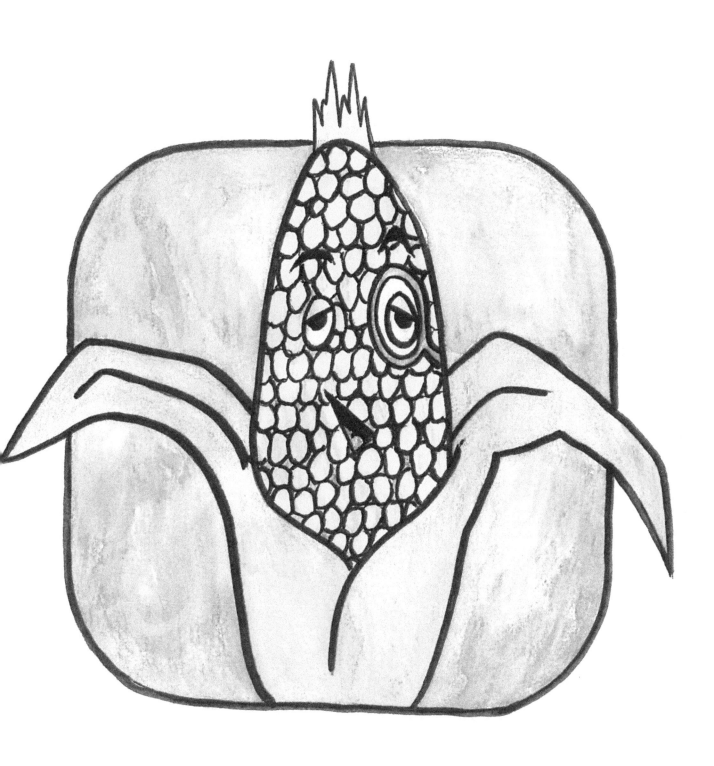

"Greens is the name. I don't have a claim to fame,
but I am glad to be here. I must be here for something
because everything under the sun has a purpose.
God created me, and I know I am not worthless."

"Well, worthless, I see, because you are taking up space for more like me."

Greens replied, "There is more than enough land to go around, and from what I can see, there's enough like thee."

"We all have a reason. It's not just your season," Greens proclaimed. "The purpose you do is being aided by everything around you."

"That may be true!" Corn yelled. "Look at what we do, from food to gas, through our growth, these things pass. So the more there is, the more corn can give."

"The parts you play, corn does not need,
because we are the special crop indeed!"

"Special is not just a label for you. God made
all of us, and we're special too. One day you
will see how we work with thee."

"So how dare you say that I'm in your way,
because without me, there may not be a you.
And potatoes and carrots, yeah, they play a part too."

The rains came, and the vegetables started to sing.
The singing was loud. Ken and Kelly were so proud,
but the rain didn't stop, and the cornfield
couldn't take another drop.

Kelly told Ken, "We did a good thing, my friend. Planting the greens when we did and having the potatoes and carrots in their place will keep a whole lot of corn from going to waste."

Corn heard their words and started to cry, "Why did I treat my neighbors so dry? Without them, there wouldn't be me. Thank God for letting them be."

About the Author

Jymi Bond is a Psychotherapist. He has a counseling practice in Colorado. The focus of his practice is Family Therapy. He has a Masters Degree in Counseling and undergraduate degrees in Social and Behavioral Sciences, and Psychology. He has an extensive background in healthcare. He has also dedicated much time as an advocate for youth. He has volunteered for many great youth organizations and projects. He was born in Macon, Georgia. *The Greens Find Their Space* is his first published work. The father of four currently lives in Colorado with his wife and their children. His venture into the writing of a children's book started with him getting ideas from his daughters at bedtime and taking one "ingredient" from each girl and turning them into an original bedtime story. From there, the idea of sharing his stories with all children began— his hope being to not only entertain but to provoke thought and educate as well.

CPSIA information can be obtained
at www.ICGtesting.com
Printed in the USA
LVHW07s0526290318
571561LV00005B/24/P